Tommy Catches a Cold

by Sarah Willson

illustrated by Barry Goldberg

SIMON SPOTLIGHT/NICKELODEON

Based on the TV series *Rugrats*® created by Arlene Klasky, Gabor Csupo, and Paul Germain as seen on NICKELODEON®

SIMON SPOTLIGHT
An imprint of Simon & Schuster
Children's Publishing Division
1230 Avenue of the Americas
New York, NY 10020

This edition published by Grolier Books.
Grolier Books is a division of Grolier Enterprises, Inc.

ISBN 0-7172-6410-6

On a cold winter day, Tommy and his friends played at the park.

Tommy waddled over to a park bench. He picked up a bottle and took a drink.

Suddenly a shadow fell over him.

"Hey! Thadz *mide!*" said a strange-looking kid with a red nose. Surprised, Tommy handed it to him.

"Hmmm," said Tommy's mother, Didi. "Dr. Lipschitz says that fresh air is good for kids, even in winter. But it looks like there are lots of children here with colds."

"Yep," agreed Betty. "Let's get the kids home before they catch one."

The next morning Tommy woke up feeling strange. His nose didn't work right. His throat tickled.

When Didi saw Tommy she panicked.

"Stu!" she called to Tommy's father. "Tommy is sick!"

"Call an ambulance!" cried Stu, rushing into Tommy's room.

"Ah, pshaw!" said Tommy's grandpa. "The little sprout just caught a bug is all."

"A bug?" Tommy muttered to himself.

"I'll call Dr. Lipschitz," said Didi.

"But it's 5:30 on a Sunday morning!" said Grandpa Lou.

Didi was already racing to the phone. She spoke for a long time, and wrote down a lot of instructions.

During the morning Tommy had to stay on the sofa. Every five minutes Didi felt his forehead and wiped his nose. Then she opened up a big purple jar.

"Just a bit of this spread on your front will help you breathe better," she said. She rubbed the awful-smelling paste on Tommy.

"Hey look, Tommy!" said Stu, coming in from the kitchen. "Your Grandma Minka brought over some old-country chicken soup. Still has the chicken feet in it!"

Later that day Tommy's friends came over. Didi made sure
Tommy was placed on the couch, far away from his friends.
"Look what I have, Tommy!" said Didi, coming into the
room with a big green suction cup.

"This will help unstuff your nose," she assured him.
"Waaaaaaah!" cried Tommy's horrified friends.
Tommy could only whimper.

"I don't thing I can take this anymore!" snuffled Tommy
miserably. "I godda find that bug and led id go!"

"What bug, Tommy?" asked Chuckie.

"The bug I caught ad the playgrowd! It must have got into
the diaper bag, but when I looked id was gone. It's gotta be in
the house somewhere!" said Tommy.

"We'll help you look for it," said Phil.

"Yeah, we'll find it," said Lil.

The babies searched everywhere.
"Is it big, Tommy?" asked Chuckie.
"Prob'ly," said Tommy.
"Should we smoosh it if we find it?" asked Lil.
"No!" said Tommy. "We gotta uncatch it! I mean, we gotta let it go!"

"Now, here's your medicine," said Didi as she returned with a cup. "I mixed in twenty-seven drops of distilled holistic oil of wheat grass into your juice. You won't even taste the medicine."

Luckily for Tommy, the phone rang. "That must be Dr. Lipschitz calling from his European lecture tour!" she said, jumping up.

While she was gone, Tommy slipped the cup of medicine to Chuckie, who hid it behind a plant.

The next day Tommy felt a tiny bit better.
"I don't know," said Didi. "He's still stuffed up.
Maybe I should call Lipschitz again."

"Nonsense!" said Grandpa Lou. "In my day we
didn't have fancy doctors—just took lots of
doses of cod-liver oil. That did the trick."

"Great idea!" said Didi, running for the
medicine cabinet.

"Keep looking for that bug!" Tommy said to his friends when they came over to visit. "I don't thing I can take any more of thad odd-liver oil."

"Cheer up, Tommy," said Chuckie. "Maybe the bug will fly away by itself."

"Hey, maybe we should open up all the windows and doors," said Phil.

"Maybe we should call the exgerminator," suggested Lil.

Suddenly Tommy's dog Spike growled. He stood stock-still as he stared at something in the corner.

"What is id, ol' boy?" Tommy whispered.

Baying loudly, Spike rushed to the corner and stopped, staring. Tommy and his friends followed. There, behind the plant, was Tommy's abandoned cup of medicine from the day before. And crawling on top of it was a tiny . . . bug.

"I don't like this one bit," said Chuckie fearfully. "That bug could be dangerous."

"Maybe we should call a growed-up," said Lil.

"Nah," said Tommy. "I caught id once, I can catch id again!"

Tommy gently trapped the bug inside his bottle.

Chuckie opened the door. Carefully, gently, Tommy set the bug free.

"Do you feel any better now?" asked Chuckie.

"Maybe a little," said Tommy.

The next morning Didi went to check up on Tommy.

"Why, Tommy, you look so much better!" she exclaimed. "And here I was coming to bring you a get-well present! It's a mobile with exotic insects from the rain forest." After fastening the mobile to his crib, Didi went to tell Stu the good news.

"Here, boy!" Tommy whispered to Spike, as he removed the mobile. "No more bugs for this baby. But I bet this'll make the perfect chew toy."

Spike stood on his hind legs and barked happily.

THE END

Now flip the book over to start another Rugrats adventure.

Didi attached a hose to the sprinkler.

"Hey, look at that! Water is coming out of the dinosaur bone!" said Tommy with surprise.

"It must be a satakite rain-making thingamajig that fell from the sky!" said Phil.

"No, it's what pirates used to make their enemies walk the plank!" said Lil.

"Oh, you babies don't know anything! It's a crown for an underwater mermaid!"

"Whatever it is, let's play!" The babies happily danced around in the water.

THE END

Now flip the book over to start another Rugrats adventure.

"Look, Didi," said Stu. He was getting ready to start the barbecue. "The kids are back. What's that thing they're carrying?"

"Gosh, it looks like an old sprinkler," said Didi. "I wonder where it came from?"

"Going home won't be so easy," grumbled Angelica. "We still have to get through this jungle. Anything could happen . . . and probably will." Phil and Lil looked worried.

The babies started back, carrying the mysterious object high above their heads. While Angelica kept a wary eye out for spiders, the Rugrats sang a little jungle-trekking song.

When they returned home, they found their parents preparing lunch.

Suddenly a big clump of dirt fell onto Angelica's face.

"Blech," she said and threw it down. "Never mind, it's just an old piece of junk."

"Space junk," said Phil. "Maybe a satakite, you know, those things that fly around in space and send pictures into the TV."

"No, it's pirate junk," said Lil. "This could be all that's left of some terrible pirate ship."

"Maybe it's a dinosaur bone," said Tommy. "Whatever it is, it's cool. Let's take it home!"

"We got it!" Phil and Lil shouted. They held the treasure above their heads. Spike jumped up and down and barked.

"But what is it?" asked Tommy.

"Can't you tell?" said Angelica. She reached for the thing and held it on her head. "It's . . . er . . . a crown, of course. Fit for a princess. It looks perfect on me. . . ."

"Let's help Spike!" said Tommy. They ran over and peered into the hole.

"Everyone, grab hold and pull," Tommy cried. "One, two, three . . . pull!" They pulled as hard as they could. When the treasure came loose, everyone went flying.

"Ouf!" said Tommy as he rolled over Phil and Lil.

"Ouch!" Angelica cried. She had stumbled into a bush.

Finally they reached the shade of the cool, green jungle. After all the excitement, everyone needed cookies and juice.

"There's nothing like a cookie after surviving a dangerous abenture," said Phil.

Suddenly Tommy asked, "Where's Spike?" They strained to see through the thick leaves. "I hope the snakes didn't get him."

"There he is!" said Phil. Spike was busy digging.

Tommy gasped. "Look! Spike's found something!"

"Wow!" said Phil and Lil together. "Maybe it's a treasure!"

"Yeah, treasure like some smelly old sock," said Angelica.

"Ugh, I got sand in my mouth," said Lil. "I need some juice."

"No snacks until we cross that desert, babies," said Angelica. "Now, crawl before this sun dries us up like raisins."

They all crawled forward through the hot sand. Only the thought of juice and cookies on the other side kept them going.

"Hey, we made it," said Tommy. He stood at the top of the mountain and looked around.

"Whoa!" Before he knew it, he was sliding down the side of the mountain. Angelica, Phil, and Lil followed close behind.

They landed—thump, thump, thump, thump—one after the other in the hot sandy desert.

The babies started up the mountain. Getting to the top wasn't easy. Spike took the lead and disappeared over the top.

"Looks like Spike found a trail," said Tommy.

"I wouldn't try to follow him," said Angelica, who was peering over the top. "There are snakes down there."

After a while, the babies stopped again.

"All right, what's everybody looking at?" said Angelica. "We'll see how all of you hold up when we cross that mountain!"

"Uh-oh," said Phil and Lil.

"Come on, guys," said Tommy. "We can do it."

They trudged along after Angelica to the foot of the mountain.

"Maybe he's found a cropodile," said Angelica. "Or a big snake. Or even a panther. You better stick close to me or who knows what might happen." Phil and Lil and Tommy were getting scared. They huddled together.

"Remember, you promised not to cry," said Angelica. "Let's get moving." But now the babies were too scared to go any further.

They plunged into the thick green branches and began their trek through the jungle. Spike ran ahead of them, sniffing.

"Do you think he smells an aminal?" Lil asked Tommy. It was kind of dark in the jungle. There were lots of scratchy branches and strange shapes.

Soon Tommy and Phil and Lil were loaded up with gear. Angelica found a backpack for each baby and filled it up with snacks and maps. She brought a hat for everyone, even Spike.

"Spike can come with us," said Angelica. "To protect us from the wild animals." The babies gulped. "Is everybody ready?"

"Tell us, *please*," begged Phil and Lil.

"Okay," Angelica said, "but if I do, promise you won't get in my way."

"We won't," Phil and Lil and Tommy promised.

"Or be scared of stuff and cry," Angelica said.

"We won't," the babies promised again.

"If I tell you," Angelica began, "and you come along, you have to do *everything* I say, because this expedition could be dangerous."

"What's an expedition, Angelica?" asked Tommy.

"A jungle trek, that's what," said Angelica. "Do you think you can handle that?" She stared hard at Tommy and Phil and Lil.

They nodded nervously.

"Hmm, I wonder if I should tell you about my expedition. Maybe I better not. I don't think it's the kind of thing babies like you would understand."

All three babies climbed out of the sandbox and crawled over to get a closer look at Angelica. Her pockets were bulging but she kept packing them with more stuff.

"What are you staring at?" Angelica asked as she finished filling her pockets.

Angelica put on a big straw hat. Tommy, Phil, and Lil watched from the sandbox. Next, Angelica put on a vest with lots and lots of pockets.

"What's she gonna do?" wondered Tommy.

"She's putting cookies in her pockets," said Phil.

"And juice boxes!" added Lil.

It was a hot summer afternoon and the babies were getting restless.

"What are you babies doing?" asked Angelica.

"We're making a big pile of sand," said Tommy.

"Do you wanna help?" Phil and Lil asked. Angelica made a face and walked away.

"I'm going to do something much more interesting than *that*," she said.

Based on the TV series *Rugrats*® created by Arlene Klasky, Gabor Csupo, and Paul Germain as seen on NICKELODEON®

SIMON SPOTLIGHT
An imprint of Simon & Schuster
Children's Publishing Division
1230 Avenue of the Americas
New York, NY 10020

Manufactured in the United States of America

This edition published by Grolier Books.
Grolier Books is a division of Grolier Enterprises, Inc.

ISBN 0-7172-8972-9

Jungle Trek

by Stephanie St. Pierre
illustrated by George Ulrich

Simon Spotlight/Nickelodeon